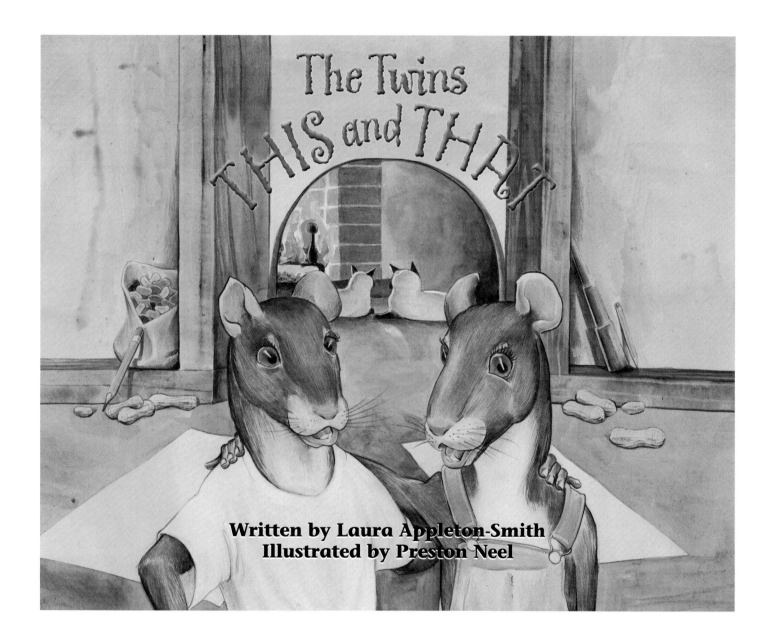

The Twins
THIS and THAT

Written by Laura Appleton-Smith
Illustrated by Preston Neel

Laura Appleton-Smith was born and raised in Vermont and holds a degree in English from Middlebury College. Laura is a primary schoolteacher who has combined her talents in creative writing and her experience in early childhood education to create *Books to Remember*. Laura lives in New Hampshire with her husband Terry.

Preston Neel was born in Macon, GA. Greatly inspired by Dr. Seuss, he decided to become an artist at the age of four. Preston's advanced art studies took place at the Academy of Art College San Francisco. Now Preston pursues his career in art with the hope of being an inspiration himself; particularly to children who want to explore their endless bounds.

A Book to Remember™

Published by Flyleaf Publishing
Post Office Box 287, Lyme, NH 03768

For orders or information, contact us at **(800) 449-7006**.
Please visit our website at **www.flyleafpublishing.com**

First Edition
Library of Congress Catalog Card Number: 2002117645
Hard cover ISBN 1-929262-15-9
Soft cover ISBN 1-929262-16-7

For Terry

LAS

⁓

For my two little pranksters

PN

THIS and THAT are twin rats
who pester and bother the Smith's cats.

The cats THICK and THIN are also twins,

but you would not think it as THICK is plump and THIN is slim.

In their nest THIS and THAT plan their cat-pestering acts.

"It will be just like a comic strip," they whisper,
"WHAM! SLIP! SPLAT!"

So as THICK and THIN nap
on their mats unsuspecting...

THAT runs up to THICK and begins to sing,
"THICK Cat, THICK Cat, you big cat...
Can you get up from that soft bath mat?"

THICK cat lifts his lids just a bit,
then THAT tugs on his whisker and runs for it.

"I smell a rat! Did you get a whiff of THAT?"
THICK asks THIN as he gets up from his mat.

THIN the slim cat is up with a jump,
he is a fast cat, set for the hunt.

This is when the rat THIS fits in the plan.
He has been sitting next to the Smith's mop stand.

As the cats run past with THAT just within grasp,
THIS thrusts the mop into their path.

Well…
The mop drops with a whack
just missing THAT's back
and stops the big cats
flat in their tracks.

Then THICK bumps into THIN with a thud and a thump
and the cats skid down the steps and land in a lump.

At the top of the steps the rats revel in their conquest.
They had out-witted the cats! The rats were the best!

But the rats
did not expect
the cats to be
back so fast.

THIN and THICK
were at the top
of the steps
and they were
mad.

"This is what
happens to rats
who disrupt
cat naps
and tug on
cats' whiskers
and drop mops
in cats' tracks!"

THIS and THAT
jump up with a gasp
and run from the cats—
they had better
run fast!

This is when the last set of twins fits in…

The kids Beth and Seth are the Smith's twins,
who had rigged up a tent from blankets and things.

Beth and Seth did not spot THIS and THAT running in,
but when the cats ran in, that was a different thing.

"Scat!" yell the twins, "Scat THICK and THIN!
You will mess-up this tent if you bump into things."

"Go back to your mats," Beth and Seth tell the cats.

THICK and THIN slink back thinking, "RATS!".

Back in their nest, just out of the grips of THIN and THICK, THIS and THAT rollick as they remember their tricks.

It was a fantastic prank, well worth the risk.

From the next nest Father Rat asks Mother Rat,
"What is that? Is it a cat?"

Mother Rat tells him, "Do not fret, Father,
it is just THIS and THAT."

The Twins THIS *and* THAT is decodable with the 26 phonetic alphabet sounds plus the "th" and "wh" phonograms, and the ability to blend those sounds together.

Puzzle Words are words used in the story that are either irregular or may have sound/spelling correspondences that the reader may not be familiar with.

The **Puzzle Word Review List** contains Puzzle Words that have been introduced in in previous books in the *Books to Remember* Series.

Please Note: If all of the words on this page are pre-taught and the reader knows the 26 phonetic alphabet sounds, plus the phonograms listed above, and has the ability to blend those sounds together, this book is 100% phonetically decodable.

Puzzle Words:
also
been
father
like
mother
worth

Puzzle Word Review List:	
a	so
are	the
as	their
be	they
begins	to
do	was
down	were
for	what
from	who
go	would
he	you
I	your
into	
is	
of	
out	

"th" words:
ba**th**
Be**th**
bo**th**er
Fa**th**er
Mo**th**er
pa**th**
Se**th**
Smi**th**'s
That
That's
then
Thick
Thin
thing
things
think
thinking
This
thrusts
thud
thump
wi**th**
wi**th**in

"wh" words:
whisper
wham
whisker
whiskers
whiff
when
whack

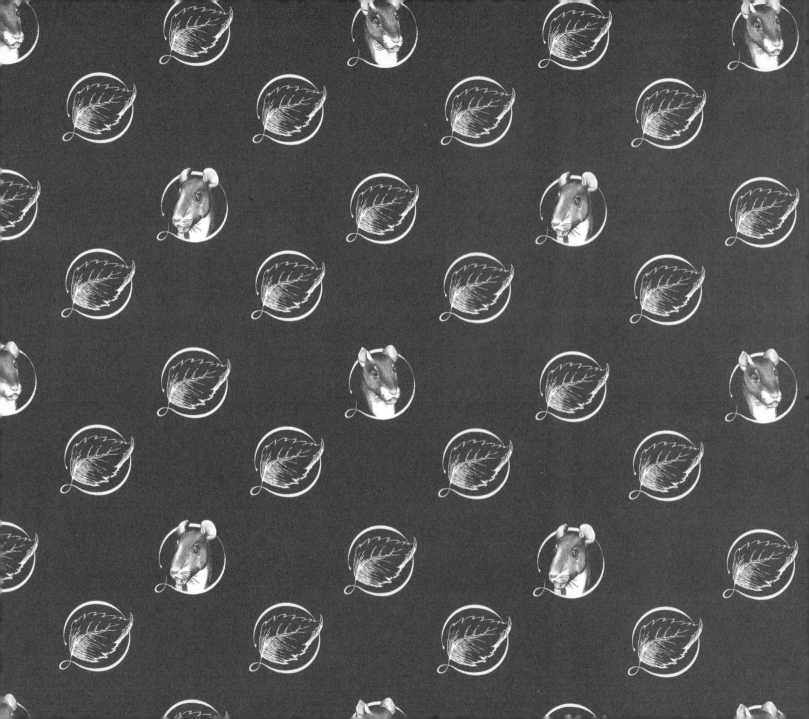